MARRYING THE BROKEN BOSS

IRIS WEST

To you, my reader. I hope you love Blossom Ford, and the sexy men, curvy women and kind but extremely interfering folk that live there, as much as I do.

CHAPTER ONE

Tiana

I RUN AS soon as the bus door opens. I hate being late. My number one rule is Do Not Be Late. Even though I know better, I ask myself why the bus had to be late today of all days when I usually can tell the time by Blossom Ford busses.

A car is coming in the opposite direction, but I figure I have enough time to cross the street. I dash across, avoiding a big puddle of water on the side of the road, but a couple of steps onto the pavement, a cold rush stops me. I glance at my front and side. They are both wet and so is part of my face and hair.

I turn around, but the car is already roaring off in the distance. A string of curses comes out of me before I can stop it. Now I'm late and messy. Even the image of Mum standing with her hands on her hips, saying she's gonna wash my mouth with soap, doesn't stop the cuss words. I set off again and sigh when I spot the humongous old house with a wrap-around porch.

I push the bell at the large gate, the butterflies that started dancing earlier this morning doing acrobatics with the added worry of my lateness and visual. I don't want my patient to think I'm a rag doll when they meet for the first time. Not patient, I correct myself, client. And a filthy rich one at that. If he takes me on as his physical therapist, he'll be my boss for the foreseeable future.

"Yes?" The voice is terse over the intercom.

"It's Tiana Remington, the physical therapist."

The intercom buzzes, and the gate swings open when I push it. I race up the long drive, fisting my free hand. I worked hard during my training period and the following years at a rehab center to know I'm very good at what I do. But this is only my second private gig, and the agency warned me to make sure I'm extra professional with Mr. cooper. There's nothing I can do about the tardiness but I have to do something about my appearance.

Near the front door, I whisk out a mirror and peer at my face and head. I get tissues from my bag and dab wet skin and hair, glad my eye liner only ran a little. There's no time to retouch my make-up. The tissue is only leaving white bits on my clothes, so I give up. I say a prayer of thanks that my top is dark blue and my trousers are even darker, then tell myself to stow away my mirror.

"Is checking your make-up when you're late part of the professionalism you mentioned in your resume?"

I gulp, feeling like a kid caught red-handedly shoving a hand into the cookie jar. I stare in the voice's direction and my breath catches. It's been a long time since I've seen such an amazing posture. A chest that makes me think the man at the door of the house must work out daily offsets straight back and square shoulders, even though he's in a wheelchair. He has green eyes, dark brown hair and a beard I want to pet. I realize I'm staring and clear my throat.

"Mr. Cooper?" Where's my usually calm voice?

"Let's get started, shall we?"

Breathe, I tell myself. I am a professional. I'm good at my job. Being turned on by a man's great posture doesn't make me weird. It's normal, cause I'm human. Also, I will not crush on my boss, I recite as I hurriedly close the distance to the door and get in the house just in time to see Mr. Cooper enter a room off the hallway.

I close the door and walk to the room. As I walk in, he doesn't take his eyes off me. Shaping my lips into my most professional smile, which makes the grumpiest of patients smile back, I hold out my hand.

"We've lost enough time. Let's begin."

I just about keep the smile in place and sit in the chair facing him, putting my bag on the floor. He's mad, I get it. I'd be mad too if I'd been as late as I am, but his rudeness is disconcerting.

"If you can't get here in time, why should I have you as my physical therapist?"

I purse my lips to stop the explanation of how I'd actually left extra early to ensure I got here early, but the bus had broken down and the next one had been late too. There was an air about Caleb Cooper that screamed of confidence, strength and self-discipline. He wouldn't care about excuses.

I look at him and make my voice strong. "I want to open a private practice by the time I'm 30. Being financially stable is crucial to me. As you will have heard from the client that recommended me, I know what I'm doing. I'm very discreet and am willing and able to carry out any other housekeeping or administrative tasks you may require. I believe those are the requisites you're looking for. There was an unavoidable circumstance today. I apologize; it won't happen again." Heartbreak over Mum and Dad's rows about money before their bitter divorce taught me the importance of money.

He searches my face for a while, then nods and interlaces his fingers over his knees.

Inside, I do a little dance of gratitude as I take out my tablet and find the files his doctor and previous physical therapist sent. I studied them last night, so I just need to ask a few questions and take down any new information before we come up with a treatment plan that'll work for him.

"What do you think is the biggest challenge to your

mobility now?" I ask and discover it's not just his posture I like. He answers my questions and asks his own with knowledge that shows he's done a great deal of research about his spinal cord injury.

CHAPTER TWO

Caleb

ARROWS OF PAIN shoot through my lower body as I take a step, then another, but I ignore them and force myself to keep going.

"That's it Caleb, you're nearly there. Keep going."

There's such a beautiful tilt to Tiana's voice. That, combined with the way she encourages me to keep going, makes me feel like there are only the two of us in the world. I want to please her, and that gives my tired body a boost.

She's walking beside me, repeating those silly words of encouragement.

"Five more steps. I'm counting with you. One, two…"

I make the last step, gripping the bars I installed in this room to help finish my rehabilitation.

"Well done! I've got you now. Put your arm on my shoulder."

I hesitate.

"Okay?"

I lift one hand off the bar and hers immediately grabs it. She puts the hand across the back of her neck and wraps her free arm around me. Tiana's tall and curvy, but her body is no match for my enormous frame and six feet-three inches, so I carry as much of my weight as I can.

She's saying something about how strong my posture is; I let her words warm me as I sit in my wheelchair.

"I'll grab a bottle of cold water," she says.

I'm exhausted, but my eyes still watch her curvy butt sway in those black yoga pants she wears. Tiana and I have worked together for five days now, and my attraction to her has only grown stronger. I've been meaning to apologize to her for the rude way I behaved when we met, but I don't know how to.

I doubt, sorry I was so attracted by the sight of you when no woman has made me the least bit interested in the last six months that I was a jerk, would work. Not when she arrives a good fifteen minutes before the start of every shift, gives her all during therapy sessions and is efficient at organizing my mail and carrying out tasks.

She's an excellent cook, too. Her meals are nutritious and meet the demands specified in her treatment plan. I've seen that drive in young men and women who became successful entrepreneurs. Once again, I wonder why money is so important to her.

Nevertheless, I have to apologize. I still can't believe I was embarrassed and took it out on a twenty-five-year-old woman. I'm nearly twenty years older than her! Before I met Tiana, the only other woman I've ever been embarrassed around is Granny.

I'm an expert on pleasing women; there is not a single woman I was ever interested in I wasn't able to charm. It looks like I lost my touch along with my mobility when I had the car accident. My lips tug up. It's no wonder I'm smiling at myself. A lot of my lovers would love to throw that bit of information at me if they found out.

Tiana strides back into the room. She hands me a water bottle and turns.

"You're welcome to stay," I say, thinking of making amends. "You can have your breaks here if you don't mind spending your free time with the boss."

A smile splits her face, stretching her almond-shaped eyes even more. "I'll get my water."

She's back a few moments later. "You're very good at your job. Sorry about the way I behaved when you turned up," I say after she sits down, cross-legged on the floor.

Chestnut colored eyes stare at me before she smiles again. I realize then that I like her eyes, too.

"I hate it when others are late too," Tiana confesses.

"This is a lovely house. I'm glad it's finally occupied and I get to be inside it. I've loved looking at it since I was little."

"My mother used to love it, too. She chose all the current furnishings and paints. When I leave for Garnet City, I'll have to think of what to do with it."

"You're not thinking of selling it, are you? It'd be a shame to lose a place like this."

There's genuine alarm in her face; it makes me curious about her. "Not soon." I love this place because I was happy here as a kid, but being here without my parents is a little hard.

"How did you know you wanted to become a physical therapist?" From a young age, I learned everything I needed to take help Granny manage our family company. Luckily for me, I loved every minute.

"When I was in junior school, we went on a school trip to the home for the elderly. A couple of physical therapists were working with some residents and I thought it was so cool, the way they could help others walk. From that day, I didn't think of being anything else."

I wish Tiana being late was the only reason I was angry at her. I tell myself I'm so attracted to her because I've abstained for too long. My body is getting fitter; it's perfectly natural to be attracted to a stunningly beautiful woman. There's nothing wrong with liking her. I've liked many of my lovers in the past.

What's worrying me is that I'm thinking of Tiana

when I wake up in the mornings. When she leaves the house for the evening, I smile at the way she said something during therapy. I look forward to her arriving for work. The sense that she brings sunshine into the dark world of pain and fear of never walking again I descended into after the accident, is increasing. That's not me. I don't do this type of liking a woman.

Her massages are supposed to relax my legs, yet her firm hands make me think about what else she can do with them. I can accept that. It's pure pleasure, something I excel in. And if Tiana weren't so young or a small-town girl that might just be looking for a relationship, a lot more would have happened between us than charged looks. Because I know women enough to tell she's attracted to me.

However, I don't do relationships. They lead to things like love. And love leads to loss so profound that makes a ten-year-old boy stop talking. The way it did when Mum and Dad died in a car accident. I never want to experience that type of pain again. Once was enough.

My phone vibrates. I pull it out of my trouser pocket and chek the name on the screen. It's Daniel, my second in command. Only he's so well-groomed at the business, he never rings unless something is massively wrong.

"Your granny's collapsed, she's in hospital right now," he says once I answer.

"Where?"

"Garnet City General. I'll organize the plane."

"Send me any details you have over the phone." I hung up, dread fisting my heart.

"Is everything okay?" Tiana asks.

"I have to fly to Garnet City. I'll call as soon as I figure out what's happening."

CHAPTER THREE

Tiana

DRIVING THROUGH RUSH hour traffic in Garnet City makes me realize how much I love the quieter streets of Blossom Ford. It's like I've left one state to go to another when both places are in Arizona. As the car approaches the hospital, I put my mask on, in case I run into reporters. But getting out of the car, into the hospital and going up the elevator to the private room Granny's in, is uneventful.

"I'm very sorry to tell you it's stage four cancer," the doctor says when I see him.

I hoped it was something as bad as a heavy cold, but this throws me. Granny's lived a long, fulfilling life, but she's the only family I have. I'm terrified of losing her.

"How are you going to treat her?"

The doctor pushes his glasses up his nose and I know

it's going to be bad.

"She's ninety-three, so operating is out of the question. Chemotherapy is going to be our best bet."

"Can you cure her?" I'm a kid clutching at straws.

"If Mrs. Cooper responds well to treatment, we can prolong her life."

By the time I finish talking to the doctor, I just want to see Granny and hug her. She is asleep when I wheel my chair into her room, after thanking the nurse who held the door open for me.

Granny looks so tiny the bed doesn't seem to have anyone in it. As I get closer, her white curls shine and I can see her face. It's smaller than the last time I saw her, which was only three days ago. When I came to live with her at the age of ten, she was huge to my younger self. Over the years, she raised and groomed me to take over the family's beauty business and only stepped down from management fifteen years ago.

"Caleb." Hearing her voice when she wakes up makes me feel a little better.

I hug her, careful not to hurt her.

"Help me sit up," she says.

"You just had to up one on me, didn't you, Mrs. Cooper?" I say after she's sitting up with her glasses on. I deliberately use the nickname I gave her when I was in high school.

"The only way to beat me is to get out of that wheelchair. How are your legs doing?"

"I'm walking short distances."

"That's really good." She caresses the blanket, taking an interest in the patterns there.

I know Granny. She has something on her mind. When she looks up at me again, the steadiness in her green eyes so like mine and the way she's holding her chin, tell me she's decided.

"I don't know how much longer I have. I want to see you settled."

I swallow. "What about all the kids I gave you?"

She laughs. "I bet you're the only grandson in the world who opens a children's centre when his granny asks for grandchildren."

"You love spending time with the kids. You're there nearly every day, it was a waste of money hiring a manager."

"I'm there to play with the kids, not manage the place."

"I'll pretend I believe that."

"Now, don't get me off topic." All amusement leaves her face, and she becomes serious again. "I don't know if I'll have time to see you holding your own babies, but I don't want to leave you alone." She puts her hand up when I open my mouth. "Don't give me that spiel about our employees being your family. This is weighing on my mind, Caleb. I want to tell your mum and dad I did alright by you."

Granny's been onto me to get married for years, but she's never mentioned my parents. It's only been six months since my car accident. Seeing the state I was in then and now finding out she's sick must have taken a toll. There's strength in her eyes; I know she'll fight this, but I can no longer deny I'll probably only have a few more years with her. If I'm terrified, she must be feeling a million times worse.

I nod.

"You'll get married?" Her voice rises with excitement.

I take her hands in mine. "Yes."

"I know a few nice girls I think you'll like."

"Whoa, hold on. I can get myself a wife."

She looks at me uncertainly. "Can you?"

I think about that question as I head back to Blossom Ford, in a small private plane owned by Cooper Beauty Industries, three days later. I can't have an actual marriage, but I want to make Granny happy. That only leaves a marriage of convenience. It's not unheard of in the circles I move in to set up a contract marriage for mutual gain.

Over the years I've heard of some elite matchmaking agencies, but Tiana's face popped into my mind as soon as the idea of a contract marriage formed. She said she needs money; she might consider my proposal. In return, I'll have a wife who'll be discreet, but so warm-hearted Granny will fall in love with her.

CHAPTER FOUR

Tiana

"HOW IS YOUR granny?" I ask Caleb. He called last night and asked to meet today.

"It's stage four cancer. She's trying to be strong, but she's worried. On top of that, she's anxious about me."

"You're doing well. If you carry on improving at your current rate, it won't be long before you walk unaided," I say when he stops talking and stares at me with an assessing glance.

"That's not her biggest worry. She wants me to get married."

"You're one of the most eligible bachelors of Garnet City. That shouldn't be a problem." I'm proud of the way my voice comes out, light, as if I'm not jealous of the prospective bride. I wonder if Caleb wants me to help organize the wedding. Or maybe he'll be shortening his physical therapy contract with me. He was supposed to recuperate in Blossom Ford for two months.

"I'm not looking to get hitched for real. So, a contract marriage is my only solution."

I frown. "You mean like a marriage of convenience?"

"Yes. Where both parties gain something."

"I see." But I don't. And why is Caleb talking about this with me?

"You mentioned you're saving up to invest in your own business. I've seen how driven you are and the way you keep working at something until you get it right; I like that. Your honesty about how money is important to you is great. I believe you're the type of girl Granny would love." He interlaces his hands on top of his knees and I follow the movement, dazed by what he's just said. "Are you interested in entering into a contract marriage with me?"

I gape at Caleb; unsure I heard him correctly. I bite my lip to stop myself from jabbering. "Are you saying you want me to be the bride in your marriage of convenience?"

"Yes."

The way Caleb says it makes it sound so simple. He's looking directly at me, cool as a cucumber, while my head is spinning. I'm glad I'm sitting down.

"I'm not sure how long the marriage will last. I'm initially looking for a three-year period with the possibility of extension on agreement by both of us. The pay is one million dollars a year plus expenses and of course, you'll be able to carry on working weekdays, with the understanding you'll have to attend enough social events to make the marriage seem real. There would be other issues to consider, but we'd have everything laid out in a contract. What do you think?"

"I'll be back in a minute, just going to get water." I force myself to walk steadily, as if I'm not freaking out by what he said.

In the kitchen, I open the freezer and stick my head in. I stay like that until I've completed three sets of counting to ten. I get a bottle of water and down half of it. Only then does my heartbeat return to its usual rhythm. Being away from Caleb's mesmerizing eyes and that beard I want to pet helps.

I make myself go over what he said calmly, thinking about this as a business. With three million dollars plus my savings, it'll be easier to open a practice. The fact I can still work is also important. I won't be able to take on anything like I did with Caleb, but I can cover a few private appointments a day. I'm already contracted to work with Caleb for two months, so I'm not letting any clients down.

It all makes sense, but I'd be living with Caleb. My heart races again. I need a little more time to think. Besides, I can't agree with anything until I've seen the rest of the terms of the contract.

I finish the bottle of water and return to the sitting

room. Caleb is still sitting where I left him.

He watches me until I'm sitting down. "Have you decided?"

"Can I see the rest of the contract first?"

"Good girl!"

The approval in Caleb's voice melts my heart and brings heat to my face. My freckles must be standing out, but there's nothing I can do about it, so I cross my legs as if his compliment didn't just shake my world.

Caleb picks up the briefcase on the floor and pulls out a set of papers. He stands up and walks the short distance to me, holds the papers out and watches me take it. It's taken effort to walk without the support of crutches and his brow is a little damp. My heart swells with admiration and respect for him all over again, and I know I'm already well on my way to falling deeply in love with him. That's why, from a non-financial point of view, this marriage of convenience might not be a good idea.

As soon as he's sitting down, I rush back to the kitchen and grab a bottle of water. Back in the room, I hand it to Caleb, then sit down to peruse the contract. I almost choke when I see sexual relations as a clause in the document. It's permissible as long as both parties consent to it.

"It seems okay. Can I have one night to think about it?"

Caleb agrees.

I think about it for the rest of the day. It's on my

mind as I talk to Mum over the phone. She's living the life she's always dreamed of, with her new Greek husband on a small island off the coast of Greece.

I turn in bed most of the night, but in the morning, as I take in my small, rented studio, I make up my mind.

"You've decided," Caleb says as soon as he opens the door, standing with the support of two crutches.

"I accept."

From that moment, everything speeds up. That afternoon, we fly to Vegas.

"Shall I hire a dress at the chapel? I'm guessing your grandma will want to see a photo of the wedding. A wedding dress will help convince her we wanted to get married," I say in the private plane flying us. I don't hide the fact that I'm enjoying the experience of comfortable seats and not having to wait in line at the airport. I'm sure this is what Cinderella must have felt like when the coach appeared at the wave of a wand.

"It's taken care of."

I sip expensive champagne to help with the butterflies somersaulting in my stomach. Deciding to take things as they come, I leave Caleb to the work he's doing on a laptop and sit back.

In Vegas, we are whisked away to a hotel in a chauffeured car. There, two women are waiting for me with a wedding dress and make up set. They help me get ready. Once they finish, I stare at the stunning, sophisticated woman in front of the mirror. The white satin dress is simple and trainless, but it fits me perfectly like it was made just for me. I'm sure my resume didn't mention my dress size, so I'm not sure how Caleb knows my size so well. My long black hair is swept up in a stylish bun, with a few curls falling down the sides of my oval face. Even my freckles appear cute.

"Ready?" Caleb asks after staring at me for what seems like ages, when I open the door to my hotel bedroom.

I nod. I've never seen him in a suit. He is handsome in a tailored three-piece pin-stripped suit. He trimmed his beard too.

He wheels his chair round and I follow him to the elevator, through the hotel lobby into a car waiting outside.

"This is Daniel Thorpe. He's my executive assistant and friend," Caleb introduces me to the man waiting there. Daniel is almost as tall and wide as Caleb with sun kissed skin and a direct but friendly gaze.

They work the brief journey to the chapel. I sit facing them. They are the two most gorgeous men I've ever seen, and it takes some self-restraint to not stare at them. Instead, I gaze at the streets of Vegas and admire the late afternoon scenery. It's my first time here and I don't know when I'll have the chance to come back.

Less than two hours later, Caleb and I are married with Daniel as a witness and are on the private plane, heading back to Blossom Ford. I must have fallen asleep because I suddenly come to when I hear him calling me.

He helps me get out of the car.

"Are you awake?"

"Yes."

If he keeps being sweet like this, I don't know how I'm going to let him go when the contract is over.

"I'm flying out to Garnet City early in the morning. Granny's being discharged. Have a good rest," he says outside my bedroom door.

I clutch my bag because his blazer is folded over the back of the chair and he's looking even sexier in his white shirt and waistcoat. I want to sit on his lap, kiss the hell out of him and touch the muscles that bunch every time he expertly turns the wheels on his chair.

"You were amazing today," Caleb says.

I blink. His voice is deeper than usual. His eyes are darker, too. He's staring at me so intently my heart speeds up. Then he breaks the spell.

He turns the wheelchair and wheels it away quickly. "See you tomorrow," he calls out.

CHAPTER FIVE

Tiana

CALEB'S BEEN AWAY for two days. He's coming back today; with his grandma. So I'm moving into his room, as per clause 8 of our contract, that states we'll sleep in separate rooms unless something happens that requires us to sleep in the same room in order to make the marriage believable.

If it were my grandmother, I'd want her to convalesce with me too instead of with a caregiver. So, I'm a little nervous but I like that he's doing the right thing by his granny.

I hear the purring sound of a car and rush to open the door. Fall night air makes me shiver.

Caleb wheels his chair to me. "Hi sweetheart. Come here." He stretches his hand out to me and when I place mine in his, he pulls me down to his lap.

I'm ready for this; Caleb warned me we'd be acting for his grandma. But I'm not ready for the way my body ignites when his fingers caress the soft skin of my nape. Or the way he ever so slowly pulls my head down, brushes my lips with his, then nuzzles my nose.

"Miss me?" he asks when he pulls back.

"A lot." My voice is croaky, I'm surprised I managed even that.

"Come and meet Granny." Caleb nudges me toward an elderly woman that looks so much like him, I realize he takes after his father's side of the family.

"Tiana, I like you already. Call me Granny. Can I hug you?"

She reaches out and I wrap my arms around her gently.

"Did you bake? I think I can smell cookies," Granny says after Caleb has seen the chauffer off and we're inside.

"I hope you like them," I say.

"I'll eat them tomorrow. I can't believe how exhausted I am after only a thirty-minute flight."

"Shall I help you get ready for bed?" I ask.

"I can manage. You should be off to somewhere exotic. I'm already feeling guilty for intruding in your honeymoon, but Caleb insisted. Now, go. Do newlywed things."

Caleb chuckles and although I blush, I can't stop my lips from tugging up.

I stop outside the room. "Do you want something to

eat?"

"I had dinner."

He heads towards his room, and I follow him. Inside, he swaps the wheelchair for crutches.

"I can sleep on the floor," I say.

"The bed is massive. It'll take both of us, unless you really want the hard floor."

I shake my head. I wash up first and get into pajamas in the bathroom. As Caleb goes into the bathroom, I get into bed, pull up the covers.

He's wearing a t-shirt and soft pants when he comes out of the bathroom, his brown hair slick from the shower. He gets into bed and switches off the bedside lamp.

"Goodnight," he says.

"Goodnight," I answer. It's a long time before my eyes close.

When I wake up, something heavy is on my tummy. Before I see what it is, I realize I rolled into the middle of the bed and so has Caleb. A slight lift of the cover shows the heavy weight is his arm.

"Do you want me to take my arm off your body?"

I turn to him. Caleb's eyes are closed. His voice is thick with sleep and something else. Then his eyes open and I fall into them.

"No. I've been thinking about this since the day I met you."

"About what?"

"You touching me. What about you?" I can sense

he's attracted to me, but I have to hear him say it. I don't want to be the only one burning. Don't want this to just be a morning crave.

"Sweetheart, I've been thinking about kissing all of you since that day, too. That's why I was such a dumbass."

A few beats later, he's still staring at me. "What are you waiting for?" I ask uncertainly.

"I want you to be sure."

My heart melts. I put my hand on top of his and move it towards my tits.

"Fuck Tiana! Do you know how much I've thought about touching these?"

I moan as he squeezes them. Then he sits up and switches on the light. "Stand up and take your clothes off. I want to see you."

I shiver at the command in his voice. I stand facing him and slowly take off my top then trousers, his eyes never leaving mine. My panties are getting wet and I'm a little embarrassed.

"Take them off and put them here." He extends his hand.

It turns out I enjoy being watched and commandeered. Another shiver runs through me. I take my black thong off, excited by the expression in his eyes. When I put it in his hand, he takes the panties to his nose, still watching me, and inhales.

"You're gorgeous, Tiana. So fucking beautiful I've been getting off thinking about you. Come here."

I'm dripping wet now, but I don't care anymore. I get in beside him.

"Lie on your back with both your arms stretched above your head."

When I've done that, he undresses, watching me the whole time. I break away from his gaze to stare at him. His chest is as beautiful as I'd imagined it. His rigid cock is reaching up toward his belly. I gulp.

Caleb stretches beside me and kisses my nose. I giggle.

"I love this pert nose and the freckles living here."

"Is that the first thing you wanted to touch?"

"Hmmm." Then his lips are on mine and he's kissing me, softly at first, then deeper until I'm gasping for breath. My arms move of their own volition and bury in his head.

"Arms back." He pulls them away and puts them back above my head. "It's been so long. If you touch me, I'll be finished. I won't last long as it is." There's an endearing, self-deprecating tone to his voice.

Caleb palms both of my tits, licks the nipples. I moan. "Fuck woman, I could worship your body the whole day. Harder?"

"Yes."

He nips them and I undulate, ready to have him inside me. He lets go of my breasts, slips one finger into my pussy.

"I'm ready." My voice is hoarse.

"For what?"

"For you to fuck me. Now."

He moves on top of me, then groans. "Shit, I want to come inside of you so badly, I forgot the rubber. Can you feel how ready I am for you?"

"Yes." His pre-cum is slippery on my thigh, mixing with my own juices.

He rummages in the bedside drawer, finds a condom, and slides it over his enormous shaft. Then he kisses me. We both cry out as he penetrates me. Caleb sets a pounding rhythm that is just what I'm craving and after only a few more thrusts, I wrap my arms around him as I come, my pussy strangling his cock.

He groans out his release and buries his head in my neck. When he's still, he rolls over until I'm lying with my head against him and his arms are around me.

I glow inside, remembering him telling me I'm beautiful. When I was in high school, I used to be so conscious about my body image, worrying all the time I wasn't as slim as most girls around my age. I did every type of diet I could find. In senior year, when one of the school's popular boys asked me to senior prom, I was over the moon. It wasn't until prom day I found out it was all a prank and he'd asked someone else to be his proper date.

After that, I swore to myself I'd let no one hurt me because of my body. If others would not love me, I was going to love myself. I ditched all my diets and, with time, learned to love myself as I was. It was funny how being self-confident actually made me more attractive;

more guys in college started asking me out. I didn't need to hear the adoration in Caleb's voice, but it gave me a warm fuzzy.

CHAPTER SIX

Caleb

"GRANNY, YOU'RE CHEATING," Tiana laughs one evening.

Just like her voice, the sound is like music; it soothes me, makes me feels like everything is alright in the world.

"How is that cheating? Honestly, young people these days don't know how to strategize," Granny grouses, but I can see the twinkle in her eyes.

We're playing monopoly in the sitting room. The pitter patter of rain sounds from outside and, together with the fire I made, makes the room cozy. I reach for my mug of cocoa and sip the hot, sweet drink. Tiana makes hot chocolate the way Mum used to make it, with marshmallows.

I hadn't had hot chocolate for decades. Yet, the

other day when Tiana was making it, the whole downstairs smelled of it and instead of sad memories, I remembered the fun I used to have with mum and dad. Tiana reminds me so much of Mum.

Two weeks have passed since Granny came to stay. Every day, Tiana has found something for us to do. Whether it's playing games, watching old movies or baking. The house feels warm and bright. Like it used to when I lived with Mum and Dad in Blossom Ford. I'd forgotten the happiness of those innocent days.

Every night, we fall asleep holding each other.

When Granny is tired of playing, we say goodnight to her and tidy up the sitting room. Tiana hates washing up, so I wash the cups while she dries. Leisurely, we head to our bedroom, hands intertwined. I started holding Tiana's hand for Granny's sake. Now it's a habit.

We make love and fall asleep, but a couple of hours later, I wake up, hard for her again. She's sleeping. I slide down the bed, gently part her legs and lazily tongue up and down the length of her clit. It's not long before she's pushing against my tongue. I keep the same pace, enjoying her sweet and tart taste.

"Caleb," her voice is thick with sleep. She runs her hands through my hair, stroking me there and even that makes me hotter. "Don't stop. Ahh, so good…"

"Come for me Tiana!"

She comes apart, her cry raw, "I love you Caleb."

I freeze. My chest tightens. I have to get away.

Tiana has fallen asleep. She's beautiful, but right now, I can't carry on looking at her. After dressing, I grab my phone, crutches and creep out of the house. I call a taxi and head for the airport. I get a first-class ticket and fly to Garnet City.

At around four in the morning, I arrive at Garnet City's Gentlemen Club. It's a member only facility that caters to the wealthiest men in the world. The place is buzzing with men playing cards and drinking. I nod to a few but head for the back room, where it's quieter and I can drink in peace.

"The usual, sir?" a waiter I recognize asks as soon as I sit down.

"A bottle."

I down the first couple of doses in one go. Tiana's words won't leave my mind. The fear they invoked is still squeezing my heart. Because I wanted to say those words right back at her. Don't really know how I stopped myself.

All these years, no woman has ever stirred my heart. I thought I was immune to love. I should have known something was wrong when Tiana was the only woman I wanted to consider for the marriage contract. Deep down, I wanted her to be mine.

"You don't look like you've found answers at the bottom of that glass."

I look up to see who's disturbing me when it must be clear I want to be alone. Blue ripped jeans and a black leather jacket are all I need to see to know it's

Alexander Royce.

"Ginger." The nickname slips off my tongue. I've been calling Alexander that since we met in Junior High. We got off on the wrong foot; it wasn't until later we became friends. By then, we were too used to our nicknames, and they stuck.

"Lass," Alexander answers and sits down. His red hair is styled differently than the last time we met.

Only Alexander could think of naming me with that ridiculous noun. He is the respected director and heir of Royce industries, a family owned multi-billion-dollar empire, but every time I see him, I can't help thinking he should live somewhere in the wilds of Africa or Australia. He said my eyes are as pretty as an Irish girl's, hence Lass.

"Do me a favor and leave me alone, will you?"

"Nah. I'm too curious. The only time you looked like this was when you thought you'd never walk again." He looks around and behind me. "You've ditched the chair. I'm impressed."

I knock back the contents of my glass and pour more. Forcing the mountain of a man in front of me to leave is pointless. "Congratulations on your marriage."

Alexander scowls. Pours himself a drink and knocks it back.

"You know it's for the merger between our two families."

I'm glad I'm not Alexander. As the CEO of our company, while I was growing up and learning the business, Granny was strict with me and always had high expectations, but I never for a moment thought she'd disown me if I failed to meet a goal she'd set. Things didn't work like that in Alexander's family.

"So, what has you hiding? You know I'm a good listener. And I always come up with solutions."

I smile at that. "I think I've fallen for a woman." The words sound strange to me.

Alexander whistles. Gives me a look of commiseration. We drink silently for a while.

"It looks like you're going to be miserable if you're away from her. At least together, you might have good times even if things go south later."

I stare at the golden liquid in my glass. If something were to happen to Tiana, what would I regret more? The pain of losing her or never loving her?

I'd hate myself for not telling her she's the only woman I want to spend the rest of my life with. I'd hate myself for not saying I love her. Even as I think this, I realize I've known it for a while now. I was just scared shitless to admit it.

I stand up. Reach for my crutches. "I'm going back to Blossom Ford."

"Say hi to August for me. I heard he got married. There's something about that small town and weddings. My future wife is from there too. And your mum."

"Maybe there's hope for you then."

Alexander grunts. A beat passes. "You're the best

man, by the way."

That is so like Alexander. Although I don't feel like it now, I'm the lively half of our friendship while he doesn't talk unless he has to. We go in different directions outside the club. It isn't possible to use the private plane right now and commercial flights are getting busier, so I head to a hotel to sober up before I return to Blossom Ford later.

CHAPTER SEVEN

Tiana

IT'S TWELVE O'CLOCK and I haven't heard from Caleb. I'm worried sick about us. When I woke, there was a note on my bedside table saying, "going to Garnet City". At first I didn't worry too much about it, but then last night came back to me. The part where I told Caleb I love him.

Technically, there isn't an us. We're simply having fun with each other while our contract lasts. In reality, I've been falling in love with him. With the way he treats Granny like losing her will take away some part of him, the way he's so focused when he works, his indomitable will to overcome his disability. I feel cherished when I'm with him and his way of loving my body, well, it literally makes me lose my mind and say things I don't mean to. I even love chatting with him.

Sometimes we stay in bed chatting about life.

I'm mad I said those three words that could rip us apart, but I couldn't help them. The question is, should I pretend it was a mistake? The contract clearly states we'll go our separate ways after the marriage is void. I wasn't supposed to develop feelings for Caleb. He was clear he wanted to remain a bachelor for life. Wearing my feelings on my sleeve will strain our relationship.

I slide a tray of chocolate chip cookies into the oven. This is the third batch. Earlier, it was oatmeal and banana.

Thinking about the ingredients for the cookies distracts me. It would have been easier to keep myself occupied if Granny were here. But she left before lunch to meet Penny, an old acquaintance she'd met while visiting Blossom Ford when Caleb's parents were alive. They were having their hair done at Raven's and were going to Jackson's Diner after for a late lunch.

Caleb's car comes up the driveway. I wait for him to come in. I get the cookie jar and slowly put away the cooled banana and oatmeal cookies. When he reaches the kitchen, I'm just finishing.

He stands in the doorway and looks at me. He's too far away for me to make out what he's thinking.

Looking at him helps me decide. I want to stay with him as long as possible, even if I'm the only one loving. Even if Caleb doesn't say he loves me, his actions and the way his eyes find me whenever he enters a room, make me feel loved.

"I'm sorry," he says.

I blink.

He leaves the crutches by the door and stalks to me. For the last week, he's been walking around the house without crutches. However, he's been on a long journey; I should assess the way he's walking, but I can't think of anything else but the look in his eyes as he gets closer. It's making me feel owned. He reaches me and hugs me tightly.

"I can't breathe," I say after a while.

"Sorry." He eases up and I'm able to wrap my arms around him.

"What's the matter?"

Caleb pushes me back a little until he's looking at me, still holding my arms. "You shared your soul with me, but I left like that. I'm sorry, I was a jackass."

"You were honest. I broke the terms of our contract."

"You weren't the only one."

He pulls my hair back from my face.

"What do you mean?"

"I love you too, Tiana. Can you forgive me for the way I walked out?"

Caleb reverently kisses my temple. The gesture is so sweet warmth spreads through me. "If you apologize like this, it'll be difficult not to forgive you."

"That's what I'm hoping for. I had the hardest time getting over my parents' deaths. I even stopped talking. Losing people I love is something I don't do well with.

My solution was not to get close to anyone. But you burrowed your way into my heart and now I can't live without you. Stay with me for as long as we both live."

"Oh, Caleb." I throw my arms around him, holding on tightly. "I will."

The oven pings, startling us. "Let me get the cookies out."

Caleb nips my lower lip before he lets me go.

"Where's Granny?"

"Out with Penny."

"Weren't they going to lunch? What time will they be back?"

"Around three, I guess."

Caleb comes up behind me, circles my waist. "We have plenty of time."

"For what?" I love teasing him.

His arms snake up my sides, and he squeezes my breasts. My smile disappears. Then he nips the soft skin between my neck and shoulder and I shiver.

He lifts the sides of my long, loose knitted dress and exposes my bare ass. "Good girl."

When he first told me to ditch panties at home, I was a little unsure, especially with Granny there. But she would never know and the way Caleb was so considerate of her, we did nothing where she might walk in on us. Which meant we always made love in the bedroom. By the end of the first day, the nerves had gone. My only concern was having a wet patch on my clothes.

Caleb kneads my ass and runs his hands up and down my thighs. I wrap one arm around his neck and turn my head to kiss him. It feels so right, the way our tongues duel together.

"Ahh, Tiana. I can't get the taste of you out of my head."

"Me too."

He rolls a nipple with one hand and with the other rubs my clit until I helplessly gyrate against him, moaning as shocks of pleasure spiral through my body.

"I love the soft way you feel against my hand when I touch you here." He gently slaps my clit before he's rubbing it again, faster this time.

I want to tell him I've always loved shaving down there, but all that comes out of me is a strangled yes as I convulse against his body, his arm holding me steady across my tits.

I'm still pulsing when Caleb leans me forward and nudges his cock against my pussy. I widen my stance, urging him.

"I want to come inside you."

"I'm safe." I press against the mushroom head of his cock and sigh when he buries himself to the hilt with a single thrust.

I wrap my arm around his neck as he fucks me leisurely, pulling almost all the way out before ramming back in and playing with my breasts until a fire is raging in my belly all over again.

"You feel so good, Tiana. Tell me you love me,"

Caleb growls against my neck.

"I love you."

"Put your hands on the counter," he rumbles.

As soon as my hands touch the surface, he grabs onto my hips and pounds against me. It's just what I need. I feel more juice come out of me, slicking Caleb's thrusts. He reaches round my hip and rubs my clit twice.

I come with a cry, arrows of pleasure shooting through every corner of my body. Caleb barks out his own release as he bucks against me.

"Are you okay?" Caleb's voice is rough from our lovemaking.

Concern has me standing upright. His recovery is progressing so well I don't want him to do any damage. "And you?"

"Let's sit before I make a fool of myself by collapsing. I think my legs will give out soon."

EPILOGUE

Caleb

One Year Later

FEAR IS A bulldozer crushing my heart. My hand is white, but I welcome the pain Tiana's crushing grip is producing. It means she's with me.

"Push," the midwife says.

The baby is a week early. This terrifies me, and I try hiding the overwhelming fear from Tiana, but it's useless. I'm looking at her and breathing with her, trying to avoid an all-out panic attack.

We take a deep breath and this time, when Tiana bears down and pushes, a cry sounds in the room. Tiana falls back on the bed, eyes closed.

"Are you okay?" My voice is so small.

I clear my throat to ask again, make sure she hears me, when she opens her eyes, smiles tiredly and squeezes my hand. She looks towards our baby, now swaddled in towels.

The midwife puts the baby in Tiana's arms. "Congratulations, you have a girl," she pronounces.

"Hello Emily Rose," Tiana whispers, then looks at me, her chestnut eyes shining with joy. "Look at our baby girl. She's perfect."

My chest is so fucking tight, I can't speak. The side of my face is strange until I realize tears are rolling down my checks. I dash them away and kiss Tiana on her cheek. Sitting beside her on the bed, I gaze at our baby girl. She's the tiniest human I've ever seen; my heart fills and I know I'm going to do everything in my power to protect her.

"Here, hold her."

Tiana places Emily Rose in my arms. I make sure my elbow is supporting her head, just like I learned in pre-natal class with Tiana. Emily opens her tiny mouth and blows a strawberry. "Hello Strawberry," I say, smiling at her.

Tiana laughs. "You can't call her Strawberry."

"Why not?"

She shakes her head. "Let's see what Granny and Mum say about it."

"She's beautiful." I can't take my eyes off her.

The senior midwife approaches me. "Let me wash her and then your family can visit."

"I'm going to sleep for a bit," Tiana says.

I hold her hand while the midwives check on her,

the baby, and tidy up the room. When they leave, they place Strawberry in my arms.

"I didn't know you'd look so handsome blowing strawberries, Mr. Cooper."

Heat spreads up my neck. "I thought you were sleeping, Mrs. Cooper." Tiana still looks tired. I hold our little girl to her. "I think she smiled at me."

She just shakes her head. "She's too young for that."

A knock sounds before the door is opened.

"Where is my namesake?" Granny says as she and Tiana's mum enter the room. Rose is Granny's first name. Granny cried when we told her if the baby were a girl, we'd name her that. I stand back as the older ladies fuss over Tiana and Strawberry.

I don't know what the future holds for us. All I can do is be stronger for the women in my life. Nine months ago, on our wedding day, I vowed to Tiana I'd live each day as it comes, that I wouldn't let my fear that something might happen at any moment prevent her from living life fully. I cheer her as she works towards opening her practice. I even promised her the three kids she wants, even though childbirth terrifies me.

I am so grateful Tiana came into my life because now I know what living is. Every single day, I'm just going to provide for my family and love them with all I have.

The End

MARRYING THE GRUMPY DIRECTOR

CURVY BRIDES OF BLOSSOM FORD #3

ALEX

I KNEW THIS day would come. I'm only surprised by two things. First, that my father let me get to my early forties before laying the foot down and insisting I do my duty to marry well and produce an heir for our conglomerate. Second, that my so-called duty is a vision of the most luscious lips and tempting curves I've ever seen. If she weren't a daughter of a family with the same money-oriented values as mine, I might believe that duty might be sweet.

But Nia is a Weston-Parker. Her ancestor was a founding member of Blossom Ford. Her family's business empire of restaurants may be a little smaller than ours, but it is as classy as their regal blood. She looks like a princess and eats like one. We're having a family pre-marriage dinner at their Michelin Star restaurant in Blossom Ford.

Our eyes meet. Hers large and the darkest brown I've ever seen. She doesn't look away; for a beat, then another, before she puts the tiniest bit of steak into a mouth I'm already having fantasies about.

I ordered a background check on her and read the dossier. But the small picture attached to the small file doesn't do her justice. She is twenty-one; the file should have been larger. Most young people in my circle do drugs, drink heavily or have some other vice.

Nia's file is clean. She spends most of her free time with a friend, hanging at the ice cream parlor, going to the cinema and the occasional night out. But I know how influential families can hide dirt, so I'm not falling for the prim way she's sitting. I'm still a little surprised that on her second college summer break, she interned at one of our hotels and received an excellent evaluation.

"Let's toast the union of our children," my father says and picks up his wineglass. "To the prosperity of both our families. May Nia and Alexander be blessed with many children to carry on our union."

Our parents beam at each other. They arranged this mutually beneficial deal. We get the Weston-Parker's five-star restaurants in our luxurious hotels while they get to have a restaurant in a third of our five-star hotels across the world.

Nia lifts her glass in salute and there's a polite

expression on her face, but she says nothing. She's a sacrificial lamb too. At least I've experienced the world, but she's fresh out of college. Even though marriages of conveniences are common in our circles, getting stuck to a man twice her age before having time to experience life fully must irritate the hell out of her.

"Why don't we let Nia and Alexander get to know each other?" Nia's mom says. Her eyes and glossy waves of hair are the only physical traits Nia inherited from her. She's slimmer and has that sophisticated look only mature women of the upper class carry.

Mother is older, but she's also slim and has that same air about her. "Alexander, why don't you take Nia to a bar? Somewhere you can have a pleasant chat." She looks at Nia. "Where's the best place to go, sweetheart?"

Nia glances at me before replying. "O'Connors, Mrs. Livingstone. It's not too far from here."

"Goodness, sweetheart! You're going to be my daughter-in-law. Call me Becky."

Nia smiles. It doesn't reach her eyes. But Mother has already turned to the vintage wine in her glass. I stand up, put my coat on, and watch Nia do the same.

"You're practically married. It's fine if you end up in a hotel room tonight." Nia's dad laughs and the other three parents join him.

"It's great to be young, isn't it?" I hear Father say as we move away from the table.

"Do you mind if we walk? The bar's only ten minutes from here," Nia says.

I shake my head. I don't understand the sudden urge to remove Nia from that room, where I know rude comments are being exchanged. Nia's parents are younger versions of mine, in looks, personality and values. I can image the bawdy conversation going on there. Though she must be used to stuff like that, I wanted to prevent her from hearing those jokes.

I thrust my hands deeper into my pockets. I can't do anything about the way my body reacts to Nia. That's biology. However, I can certainly control these feelings of protectiveness and empathy towards her. I'm not letting a woman into my heart again.

Though it's been thirty years, Mother's words are still as clear as the day she uttered them when I caught her making out with another man in our hotel suite, her bra strap half-way down her arm.

"What Mom and that man were doing is perfectly normal. Dad is doing it with other women. That's how the world is. Now, go back to sleep." She'd pushed me towards my room. I couldn't sleep and put a pillow over my head to escape the noises she and the man were making. What they were doing seemed wrong. I couldn't stop myself from thinking I had a bad Mom.

Years later, I learned what my parents did was a choice, but by then I'd stopped believing my family could be like the happy families in movies. I stopped hoping Mom, as I used to call her when I was little, would come pick me up after school like some of the other moms did. I stopped hoping for Sunday family picnics and got used to eating perfectly healthy meals alone.

Whatever this feeling towards Nia is, I'm stopping it before it takes root. Although Father is the CEO of Livingstone Enterprises, I've taken over most of his work for the foreseeable future while he recuperates from a heart attack. Thousands of employees depend on the success of our hotels and subsidiary companies. That's where my focus should be

We walk quietly along Blossom Ford's Main Street, accompanied by the silvery moon, a gentle fall wind and the occasional shout from passersby exiting buildings. I make myself think about the new hotel we're opening in the West side of Blossom Ford, by the mountains, and focus ahead, away from the sway of Nia's hips.

"I'm sure you have things to do. Let's finish these drinks, then go our separate ways," I say after placing a pink gin and tonic in front of her at a corner table in the modern bar. O'Connors is buzzing with people from all ages and walks of life, enjoying drinks on a Sunday evening.

"I thought we could spend a little time together." She plays with the straw in her glass.

What does she mean? "Is there anything you'd like to know?"

Nia takes a long pull on the straw, her eyes facing the cup. "Not anything in particular."

"Did you read the marriage contract?" I don't want

to listen to complaints about the contents of the contract later.

She sits up straighter. Tears her eyes from the gin and looks at me. "I did."

"Good. Do you want to wait a little before trying out for a baby? That's the only thing we have to decide on."

"What do you think?"

I'm used to people being intimidated by me, especially youthful women. But Nia doesn't cower from me. I like it.

Stop thinking about things like this, I tell myself. I can feel the frown forming on my brow.

"It's better to get it done. Then you can have your freedom." My voice is rougher than usual, but the thought of a little boy or girl wanting a hug from their absentee mom tears at me. No matter what kind of mother Nia turns out to be, I'm going to give my child all the affection in me.

She takes a moment to answer. Then, "I agree. There's a five-year term to fulfill the heir condition, but it's impossible to guarantee pregnancy. The sooner we start, the better."

God, the thought of getting her pregnant is making me hard. I drown the contents of my glass. "Are you ready?" Her glass is only half-empty, so I know I'm being a dick, even as I say the words. But I can't believe those emotionless words are coming from that kissable mouth.

"I'm done."

MATCHED TO PATRICK

THE O'CONNORS OF BLOSSOM FORD #1

PATRICK

MINGLED LAUGHTER DRIFTS from the sitting room, bringing mixed feelings of joy and sadness. We decorated the entire house in green–it's St Patrick's Day. As usual, we've been to church and are now having beef pot roast, which Mom and Aunt Shauna insist on making every year on the feast day of St. Patrick. Dad would have been so happy to hear that laughter. Even though we gathered like today at Christmas, St Patrick's Day was his favorite holiday.

I remove more salad from the refrigerator.

"Ready for the parade of women our moms no doubt have lined up for you this year?" My cousin Lorcan asks. I know his lilting voice like I know my own.

I snap the refrigerator closed. "Will I be the only one on display?"

He winces. "You're the eldest. And you're Aunt Caitlin's only son, so you'll definitely be in the firing line. Mom will surely want to marry Riordan off first. I'll be an afterthought."

The lump in my throat prevents me from chuckling. I can't really blame Lorcan. I used to be like him. The thought of marriage drove me barmy. Not anymore.

At first I couldn't imagine myself being happy with a family, not with the crushing guilt I felt over what happened to Little Fiona. Before Dad passed, he made me promise to let go of that guilt and cherish the time I've been blessed with. Although I believed it'd never happen, little by little, I'm appreciating life.

I want what Mom and Dad had, though. They were meant for each other. Someone out there is my soulmate and the moment I find her, I'm not letting go. For the last couple of years, Mom and Aunt Shauna's matchmaking efforts haven't bothered me in the least.

I glance outside to where Riordan, my cousin and Lorcan's eldest brother, sits in the spring sun. "Riordan is not ready to get married. I doubt he'll hang around for the picnic and anyone our moms might want to set him up with."

That giant of a man is still blaming himself for what happened to his little sister Fiona, even though it's been twenty-six years since she was taken from us. Our dads were first cousins -both O'Connors. The two of us are forty-four, but I'm older than Riordan by one week. As the oldest children in the O'Connor family, it was our responsibility to make sure Fiona was safe.

Lorcan opens the back door.

"Mom is calling," he says to Rio.

It's the only thing that'll move my eldest cousin. Aunt Shauna may not be calling him now, but Riordan knows she'll soon be, wanting to make sure he spends as much time with us as possible before he scoots up the mountain.

Riordan and Lorcan's six brothers and Dad are watching TV while Mom and Aunt Shauna are chat.

"Don't forget to take good care of my friend Nara when she gets here. She was very kind to me the other day in town when I forgot my wallet," Mom reminds me.

We spend another couple of hours leisurely drinking and chatting, then get up to prepare for the outdoor picnic, which starts at four. The whole town is invited to our farm. Our parents started the tradition a few years after settling in Blossom Ford and starting a lettuce farm together, because they missed spending St Patrick's Day with their large family back in Ireland.

We put up tents on the large grass area between my house and Riordan's. Mom and Aunt Shauna used to do all the food when they were younger, but now, Lorcan gets caterers in to bring sandwiches and other finger food. By the time the townsfolk arrive, Cormac and Emmet, my youngest cousins, have set up a DJ stand which is playing upbeat music and the entire field is filled with green bunting and balloons.

I'm taking a breather from greeting people when I see a woman strolling towards Mom. Something about the way she walks catches my attention. She's wearing black skinny jeans that mold her curvy ass to perfection and a light green top that covers a pair of generous breasts and complements the sun-kissed tone of her skin. Wavy jet-black hair falls below her shoulders and shimmers in the sun.

I'm too far away to see the color of her eyes. Before I know it, I'm marching towards Mom, curiosity and something I can't name, compelling me forward.

"I'm so glad you came, Nara," Mom is saying when I reach her side on a strategic part of the field where she, Aunt Shauna, and their friend Ms. Penny can see everyone.

Tawny, that's the color of her eyes.

I answer myself as Nara greets everyone with an amiable smile that reaches her almond-shaped, yellow-brown eyes and warms the inside of my chest. She's comfortable around Mom, Aunt Shauna and their friends, even though she must be in her mid-twenties. The silver hoops on the tops of her ears glint in the sunshine.

"This is my son, Patrick." Mom points to me.

I stretch out my hand in greeting and when she holds mine; hers is small and smooth against my large and calloused one. I don't let go and she glances up at me.

That's when I know. That I've found the woman I've spent the last few years searching for.

The friendly warmth on her face is replaced by something else: interest. A tinge of pink fills her cheeks before she pulls her hand away.

Her voice cracks a little when she says hello leaving me to wonder where the confidence she exhibited a few moments ago went.

"I'll show you where the food is," I say.

"I don't want to trouble you." She looks about her. "I'll find it, thank you."

"It's no trouble at all," Mom beams at Nara. "Patrick will walk you over to the food area. Just ask him if there's anything you need to know."

A frown forms on my face as I lead the way. At my age, I'm old enough to know when a woman has the hots for me. I know Nara fancies me, but she's decided not to pursue it.

If there's one thing I'm good at, is getting to the root of a problem. Now I've found Nara, I'll have to convince her I'm the only man for her.

OTHER BOOKS BY THE AUTHOR

CURVY BRIDES OF BLOSSOM FORD SERIES

MARRYING THE PROTECTIVE PROFESSOR

MARRYING THE GRUMPY DIRECTOR

MARRYING THE POSSESSIVE NEIGHBOR

MARRYING THE WIDOWED DOCTOR

MARRYING THE SCARRED SOLDIER

MARRYING THE OBSESSIVE CEO

MARRYING THE BIG MOUNTAIN MAN

THE O'CONNORS OF BLOSSOM FORD SERIES

MATCHED TO PATRICK

ABOUT THE AUTHOR

Iris West writes short and spicy romance about alpha heroes and the women they can't help falling in love with. She loves reading all types of romance books that have a happy ending and is an avid Kdrama fan.

Follow or like her on Facebook and Goodreads.

FREE BOOK

Would you like a free book? Sign up to my mailing list at https://dl.bookfunnel.com/t191w45ryj to receive a copy of Loving My Fake Husband, a free to subscribers only, Curvy Brides of Blossom Ford Series short story.

HELP OTHERS FIND THIS BOOK

Thank you for reading Marrying The Protective Professor. If you enjoyed this book, please help others discover it by leaving a review at your favorite online book store.

Many thanks,

Iris xx